GRAFFIX

First paperback edition 2000
First published 1999 in hardback by
A & C Black (Publishers) Ltd
35 Bedford Row, London WC1R 4JH

ISBN 0-7136-5098-2

A CIP catalogue for this book is available from
the British Library.

Printed and bound in Spain by G. Z. Printek, Bilbao.

The Haunted Surfboard

Anthony Masters

Illustrated by Peter Dennis

A & C Black · London

Chapter One

Jack Morton raced after his classmate, yelling furiously.

Give it back! Give it back!

Make me.

Come on. Make me.

Jack didn't really want to get into a fight but there didn't seem much alternative. Darren had grabbed his lunch box and didn't look like giving it back.

Jack threw himself at Darren, knocking the lunch box to the ground. As the two boys fought, they over-balanced, and were soon rolling about on the floor.

Mr Dawkins, their form tutor, was there in seconds.

As Darren went off with his mates,
Mr Dawkins took Jack aside.

You're not making friends very easily, are you?

Mr Dawkins smiled, not wanting to be too hard on him. He knew that Jack's parents had recently split up and that his mother had moved to Cornwall to make a fresh start.

No one likes me here.

But I don't care.
Everyone in Cornwall's soft.
I used to be a hard guy in London.

Mr Dawkins sighed.

Jack picked up his lunch box and walked slowly away. He missed his dad and he missed London. Why had Mum dragged him down to this dump?

But the dump had waves.

That evening Jack forgot all about his problems at school as he paddled out to sea on his surfboard.

There was no one else around and Jack was disappointed. He did want to make friends. Even if the school kids wouldn't accept him, surely the surfers would. But the beach was long and lonely and, as usual, deserted.

Jack sat on his board staring out to sea. As he waited for a good wave he thought about his fight with Darren.

Will I ever make friends?

Then he saw the wave rolling up.

He waited excitedly for the right moment to make his move.

With expert timing, Jack caught the roller and stood up on his board. He rode the crest, his heart thumping with excitement as the wave carried him in.

As Jack turned to paddle back out he noticed a boy surfing near the rocks.

But the thundering of the surf was far too loud for the boy to hear.

Jack was puzzled. Where had the boy come from? He glanced back at the summer cottages at the head of the beach. It was early May and his was the only one let.

Then he saw his mother walking down the beach towards him.

Time for tea.

That boy - he's in trouble.

Which boy?

Out by the rocks.

His mother gazed out to sea.

I don't see anyone.

But Jack was already pushing
his board through the shallows.

Get help, Mum.

As she ran towards
the cottage, Jack
straddled his board
and began to paddle
towards the rocks.

Chaper Two

Jack approached the rocks cautiously, trying not to be drawn towards them by the current and the pounding breakers.

But when he got nearer, Jack could see no sign of the boy at all. He seemed to have vanished without trace.

Where are you?

I've come to help.

Jack tried to paddle away again, but with sudden panic realised the tide was sweeping him into a narrow channel.

All he could see was spray and sharp barnacle-encrusted rocks that he knew could rip him to pieces.

What am I going to do?

He had to make a decision. But the panic swept over him like the waves and Jack couldn't think what to do as he was driven even nearer the deadly reef.

Suddenly Jack saw the ledge above him. He grabbed at a mass of seaweed, kicked away his board and managed to pull himself up.

Where are you?

I've come to help. Now you'll have to help me.

Then with relief he saw someone swimming towards him, and through the spray saw a jeep on the beach. It was a lifeguard, responding to his mother's emergency call.

21

Is it worth it?

The lifeguard glanced to the right and Jack followed his gaze. His board was rammed into a cleft in the rock and had broken in two.

I'm sorry.

So am I.

I'll never be able to afford another one.

Once the lifeguard had got him back to the beach and delivered another safety lecture, he drove off, leaving Mrs Morton angry and humiliated.

Of all the stupid, irresponsible things to do. You could have drowned out there.

I saw this boy.

No one else did.

Chapter Three

The next evening, with the surf riding high, Jack walked gloomily down the beach.

If only I had a board. I'll never be able to save up enough money to buy one this summer.

Jack sat down and gazed out to sea. He felt desperately sorry for himself. Dad had given him the board just before he left home and it was very precious to him.

Suddenly something in the water caught his eye. It was floating away from the rocks. At first he wasn't sure what it was.

Is it a dead body? No, too flat.

Could it be a surfboard?

Jack watched as it caught the crest of a wave and hurtled towards him, landing in the shallows.

Jack made a dash for it, pulling the board up the sand. The surfboard was old and battered but beautifully waxed. Jack looked around. There was no one in sight, so he picked it up and headed for home.

His Mum was not at all pleased to see the surfboard.

It just floated in towards me.

But it doesn't belong to you!

Jack knew that she didn't want him
to go back into the sea.

Look, Mum - if anyone claims this board
I'll give it back to them. I promise.

Mrs Morton gazed at her son doubtfully.

The next day was Sunday and the light and the surf were perfect.

A boy was surfing dangerously near the rocks and he had long, blond hair.

Surely this isn't another trick of the light.

As Jack ran down the beach, however, he felt very lonely, wishing he had a friend to surf with. Then he came to a sudden halt.

Jack began to feel cold inside.

He paddled out beyond the breakers and watched. Jack could see the boy very clearly in the strong sunshine.

After a few seconds the boy caught sight of Jack and came swiftly towards him.

Where did you get that board?

I found it on the beach.

Let's have a proper look.

Reluctantly, Jack paddled back through the surf and into the shallows, followed by the boy.

Jack felt uneasy. This stranger was identical to the boy he had seen yesterday. Was it all some kind of mistake?

Weren't you out at the rocks yesterday?

What do you mean?

The boy looked afraid.

You were surfing near Crab Rock - too near. I paddled out to warn you - but you disappeared.

It wasn't me.

The boy looked even more afraid now.

The boy watched as Jack dragged the board up the beach.

Jack decided not to tell him that the board had floated in from the direction of the rocks.

I know it's my brother's.

Has it got his name on?

The boy examined the board carefully.

It must have got rubbed off.

Then how do you know it belonged to him?

Jack knew he sounded aggressive but he was worried that the boy was going to try and take the board away from him.

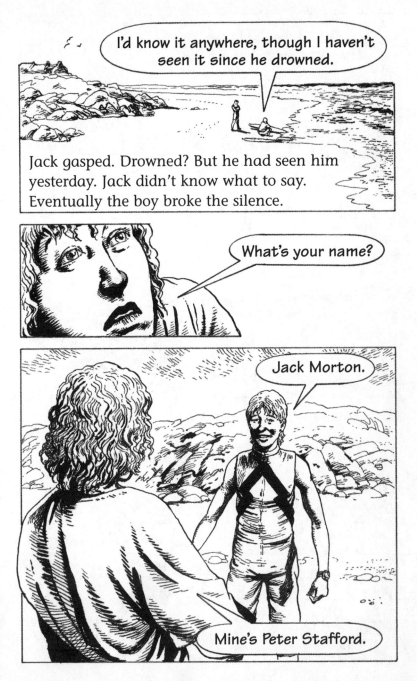

I'd know it anywhere, though I haven't seen it since he drowned.

Jack gasped. Drowned? But he had seen him yesterday. Jack didn't know what to say. Eventually the boy broke the silence.

What's your name?

Jack Morton.

Mine's Peter Stafford.

Peter shrugged. There seemed to be nothing to say.

Because my brother ignored them too. Tom was a real dare-devil. He was determined to surf Crab Rock. But he drowned doing it.

Peter was still gazing down at the board.

It's so weird this has turned up after all these months.

Perhaps it got wedged somewhere.

Maybe. But why are you fool enough to try and surf Crab Rock? After what happened to your twin?

They both gazed out at Crab Rock.

That's a risk I'm going to have to take.

When the surf's high enough I'm going to give it a try.

Chapter Four

That night, Jack told his mother about Peter.

I've made a friend.

Who is it?

Peter Stafford. He's staying in the cottage next door. His brother drowned here last year.

Mrs Morton gave Jack a strange look.

Is he the boy that's been risking his life out there?

He knows what he's doing.

Does he? I'd rather you didn't make a friend of him.

Why not?

He's too much of a dare-devil.

Before he went to bed that night, Jack opened his bedroom window and watched the surf gleam in the moonlight. He knew that what Peter was planning was very dangerous. He could drown. But Jack was glad to have made a friend at last.

41

Later that night a huge storm broke. Jack's mother came rushing into his room looking terrified.

I've never seen the surf so high. Do you think we're going to be flooded?

They huddled together at Jack's bedroom window, watching the huge waves breaking. The tide was creeping nearer and nearer the cottage. The spray rose as high as the chimney, and the long fingers of water reached right into their garden.

Jack gazed down at the next-door cottage. Peter had left the surfboard just under the kitchen window but now it was floating down the garden.

I've got to save that board.

Jack ran to his bedroom door.

You'll drown!

I'll be careful, Mum.
I've got to keep that board safe.

As Jack ran out into the surf-swept garden he saw
Peter coming out of his back door.

The board was on a patch of sand. The wave hadn't been quite strong enough to drag it out but there was another on the way.

We'll have to leave it!

No. I'll get it.

You wait here.

Jack had always been a fast runner. Now he had to be just that little bit faster. The next huge wave was surging towards him.

But Jack had already gone.

Jack sprinted across the wet sand towards the board, knowing the wave was already breaking. Any second now, the surf would be hurtling towards him.

He just managed to grab the edge of the board as the surf hit him. In dismay, Jack felt the wet surface slip out of his hand and the board being jerked away, almost as if someone was pulling at it.

Then, suddenly, he was knocked sideways, as if an unseen hand had pushed him out of the way.

Seconds later, he found himself rolling over on wet sand.

Run! or the next wave will get you!

Jack struggled to his feet and raced after Peter.

Follow me!

They ran up the beach and just managed to reach the safety of the cottages before the next wave shot spray into the garden.

51

Jack ran back home, knowing that he was in for a telling off. His Mum was waiting for him at the door.

53

At least Jack could be honest about that.

54

Chapter Five

The next morning, Jack opened the window and was amazed to see the surfboard lying outside.

Peter's voice spoke again in his mind.

I reckon Tom's playing games with us.
He was like that.
Always teasing.

Jack crept down the stairs and cautiously opened the front door. As he grabbed the board it seemed to move in his hands. Maybe Tom was just playing games.

Jack gazed out at the surf.

Are you out there, Tom? Are you trapped?

Suddenly it didn't seem to matter to Jack that the surf wasn't high enough or about the promise he'd made his mum.

He turned to Crab Rock and whispered:

Are you out there, Tom?
I'll show you how it's done.

For a moment Jack thought he heard a mocking whisper in the wind.

Will you now?

Hoping his mother was still asleep, Jack put on his wetsuit, picked up the surfboard and ran down the beach towards the surf.

Seconds later he heard feet pounding on the sand behind him. He turned and saw Peter running towards him.

Where do you think you're going?

I thought I'd try the rock.

That's my job.

Suddenly the board flipped over, its keel almost hitting Jack's knee. Peter made a grab for it.

He held on to the board but again it flipped over, this time cracking him across the shins.
He leapt back in pain.

The board lay on the sand between them. With a sudden lunge, Peter made another grab for it and then backed off with a sharp cry.

What happened?

It's given me a splinter in the palm of my hand.

Let me have a look.

Peter gave a howl of pain as Jack pulled it out.

Now I'm bleeding.

You'll live.
Wait a minute, though.

What is it?

63

They looked out to sea. The surf was lashing Crab Rock and the spray was rising up into the early morning sky.

I don't think the surf's high enough.

It'll have to be. I want to get it over.

You don't think Tom - wants you to join him?

Wants me to drown too? No - he wasn't like that.

Peter sounded confident.

Not like that at all.

Chapter Six

As Peter paddled out into the surf with Jack swimming behind him, the sun came out, turning the waves golden. Peter positioned himself close to Crab Rock, and waited for a wave of the right height.

Jack watched him from a safe distance.

He's having to wait a long time. None of the waves are big enough.

Peter was about to reply when he saw a huge wave in the distance. Jack saw it too. If Peter could only get on its crest, then he was in with a chance.

Jack watched the roller coming in.

Then, at just the right moment, Peter caught the wave and was up on his feet. Jack could hardly bear to watch as the crest soared above Crab Rock with Peter balancing on Tom's board, just clearing the barnacle-covered surface.

Peter was gliding towards the shore now, still on the wave, cheering and clapping. Then, for no reason, he fell off his board. But, to Jack, it looked as if someone had pushed him.

Jack swam towards Peter in a fast crawl, pushing himself harder than he had ever done before, but he knew he wasn't making enough progress.

As Peter struggled in the current,
Jack saw him go under.

Hang on!
I'm coming.
Just hang on.

But although Peter bobbed up and swam a few more
feeble strokes, he soon went under again.

Jack pulled at the waves, his muscles screaming, but
when he looked up Peter was even further away.

Jack was trying to be brave, to sound more confident than he felt. Peter was being dragged further and further away. He'd drown if Jack didn't reach him soon.

Suddenly the waves around Jack turned golden, and although the crests hadn't broken, spray leapt into the air and began to make a human shape. It hung just above the surface of the sea.

Jack was completely dazzled by the figure. He screwed up his eyes against the brilliance, going under and swallowing salt water as he did so. As he surfaced he yelled to Peter.

Hang on! I'll be with you in a moment.

Jack watched as the sparkling figure with the shock of blond hair stood up on the old board and headed towards Peter. Peter was still struggling, each stroke weaker than the last, unaware that help was so close at hand.

Then Tom bent down and with easy strength pulled Peter up on to the old board.

I surfed Crab Rock. Did you see me, Tom? You're free now. Free to go.

Watching intently, Jack saw Tom move slightly to the rear of the board, his spectral body shimmering in the golden surf.

Then they caught a wave which gently took them into shallow water.

Suddenly another wave broke and Jack was carried towards the beach in a sheet of spray. As he headed towards the shore, Tom's sparkling figure passed him, going the other way, without the board.

His feet were balanced on a wave
that was running in the wrong direction,
sending him hurtling towards the horizon.

But Peter insisted.

He'd want you to have it,

so we can go surfing together.

Jack grinned and they both gazed out to sea as the surf came thundering in.